Solar System Forecast

by Kelly Kizer Whitt

illustrated by Laurie Allen Klein

Good morning space explorers! This is your weatherman with today's solar system forecast: hot, cold, windy, calm, rainy, dry, cloudy, clear, and everything in between!

Let's take a closer look at the details . . .

The Sun is active today, with dark sunspots scattered across the surface like polka dots. These holes in the Sun's surface are churning storms. Gas shoots out of these dark holes and flies out on the solar wind, making exploration dangerous. We do not recommend travel.

DEPARTURES

123	Mercury	CANCELLED
526	Venus	CANCELLED
1538	Earth	CANCELLED
7490	Mars	CANCELLED

solar flare
sunspots
TRAVEL ADVISORY
SOLAR
WEATHER
CHANNEL

Mercury is so close to the Sun that almost its entire atmosphere has been blown away by the solar wind. With no air, this planet has wild temperature swings. It will get up to 800°F during the day. Pack something warm for night when temperatures drop to -279°F.

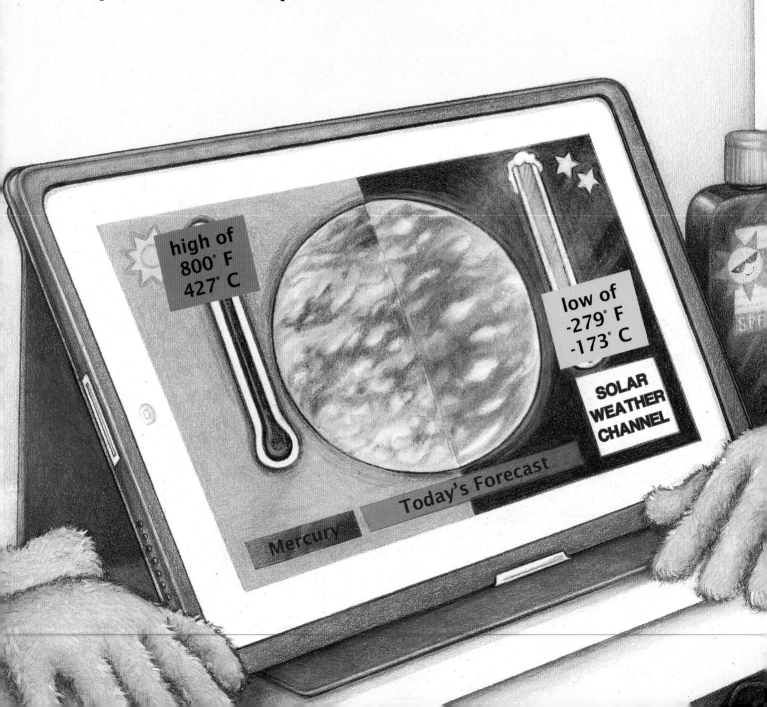

Expect thick, yellow sulfuric acid clouds on Venus today . . . and every day. These clouds trap the Sun's heat with a constant greenhouse effect.

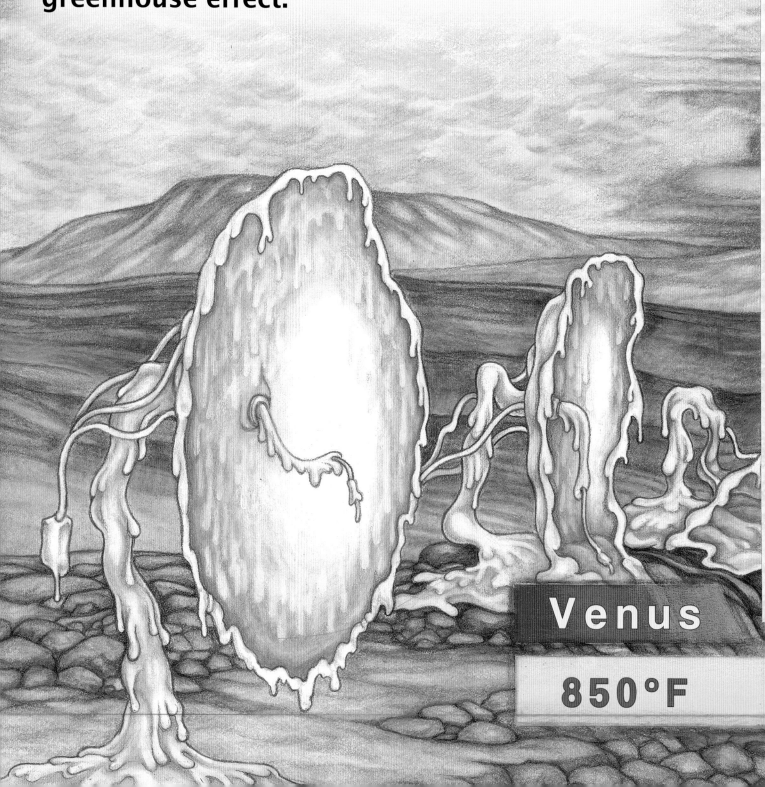

Venus

850°F

Earth is the Goldilocks planet: not too hot, not too cold, its nitrogen and oxygen atmosphere-based climate is just right! It is cold at the poles and warm at the equator. Travelers should avoid the western Atlantic Ocean today where a hurricane is raging. Afternoon storms are possible in some areas.

If you visit Mars today to catch one of its famous pink sunsets, watch out for dust devils spinning like little tornadoes across the rust-colored surface.

Storm chasers should head on over to Jupiter, where they are sure to nab a big one. The Great Red Spot is a storm that has been raging since Jupiter was first viewed through a telescope 400 years ago. It is the size of three Earths! Keep an eye out for junior-sized storms nearby.

SOLAR WEATHER CHANNEL

Storm Chaser Update

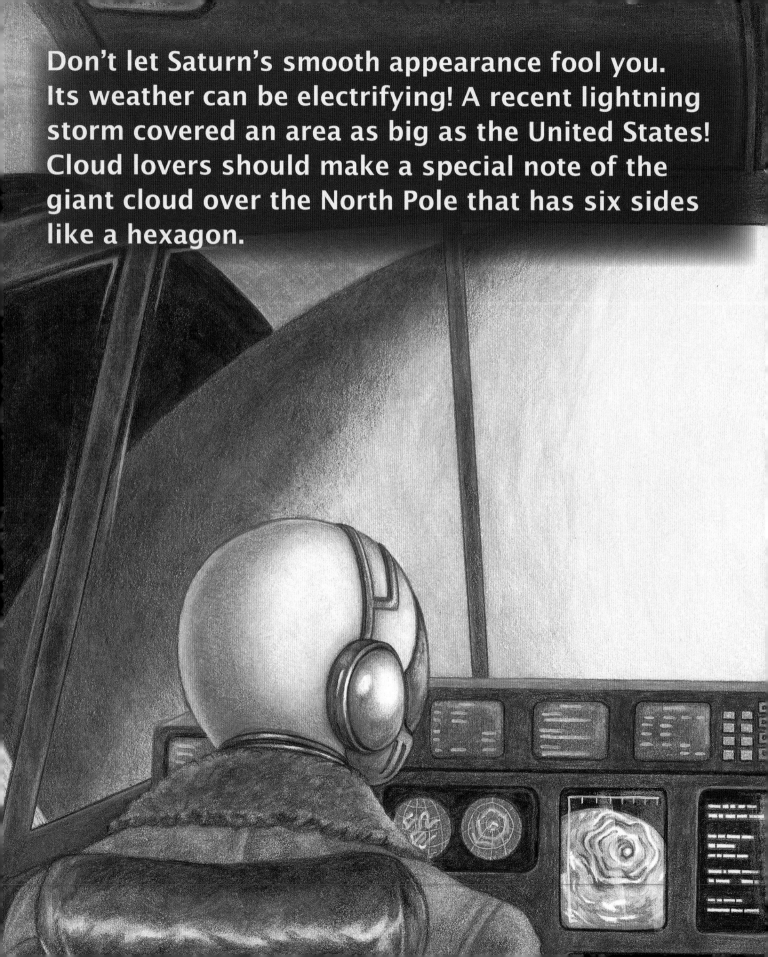

Don't let Saturn's smooth appearance fool you. Its weather can be electrifying! A recent lightning storm covered an area as big as the United States! Cloud lovers should make a special note of the giant cloud over the North Pole that has six sides like a hexagon.

There are at least 170 moons throughout the solar system. Only one has a thick, hazy atmosphere— Saturn's largest moon, Titan. Just like Earth, the main gas in Titan's atmosphere is nitrogen. But if you visit, make sure you take your jacket and an umbrella. Titan has a 100% chance of methane-rain drizzle today!

Looking for calm weather? Try Uranus. One Uranus year lasts as long as 84 Earth years. Most of its stormy weather happens during the season changes—about every 21 Earth years. Spring came to Uranus a few years ago and will last until 2027!

Hang on to your hats if you're visiting Neptune. With winds up to 1,500 miles per hour, this is the windiest planet in the solar system. The methane gas in its below-freezing atmosphere gives Neptune its beautiful blue color.

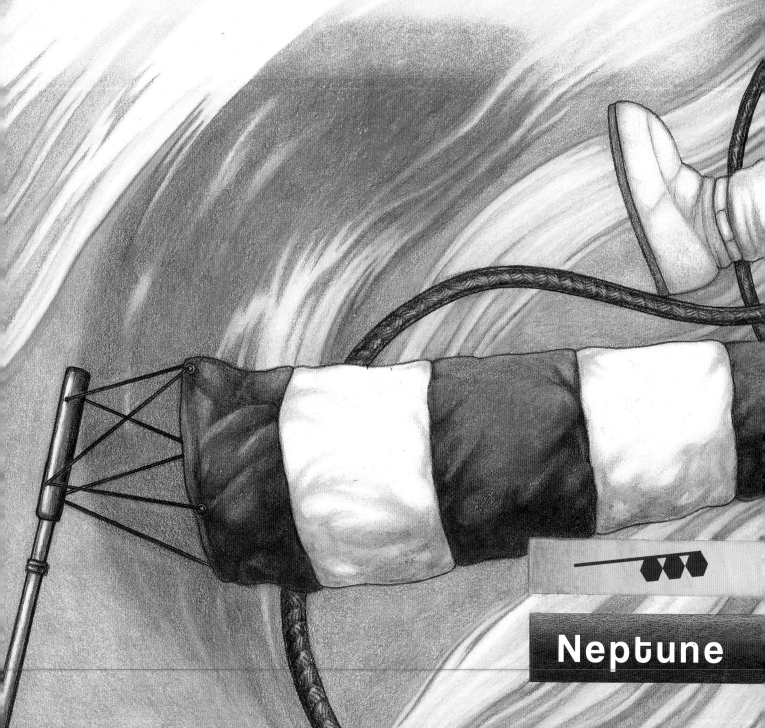

Neptune

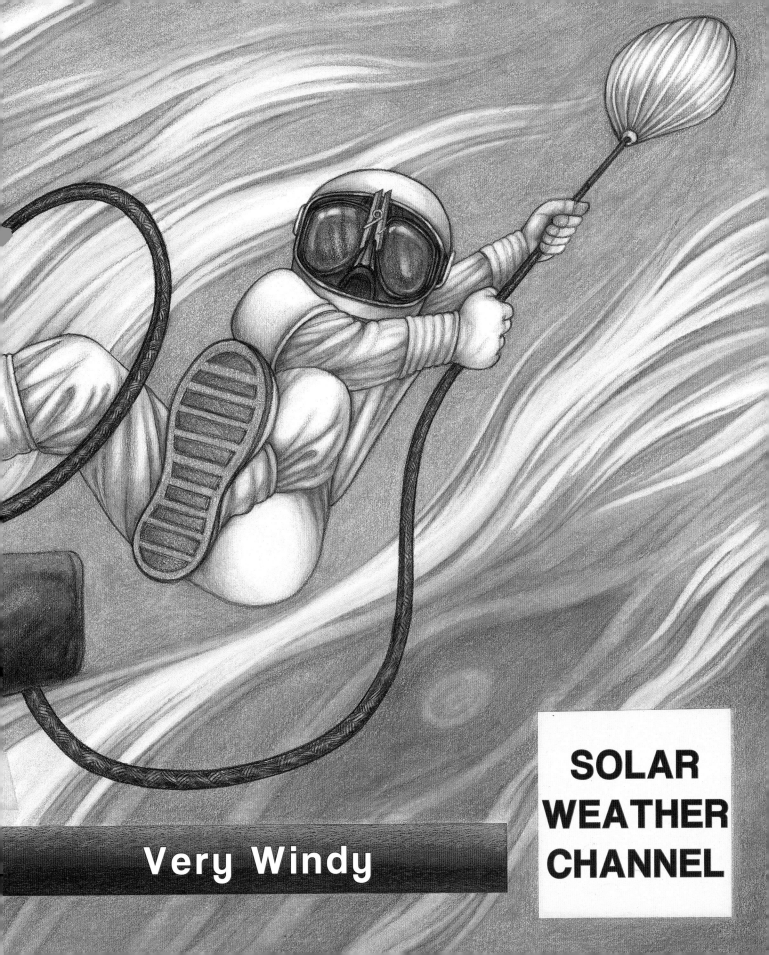

Very Windy

SOLAR
WEATHER
CHANNEL

Pluto's atmosphere is freezing and falling to the ground like snow. Clear skies should return as Pluto moves even further away from the Sun on its oval orbit and the atmosphere has completely frozen and fallen to the ground.

For Creative Minds

Solar System Compare and Contrast

Compare and contrast the different solar system objects mentioned in the book.

Scientists had different understandings of what a planet was. In 2006, a group of scientists from all over the world (the International Astronomical Union) defined a planet as an object that orbits a star, has an almost round shape, with no other objects of the same or smaller size in its orbit other than its own moons (satellites).

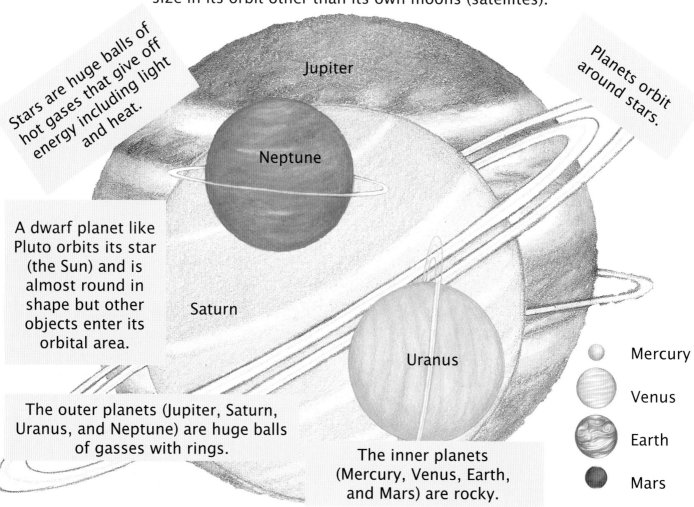

Stars are huge balls of hot gases that give off energy including light and heat.

Planets orbit around stars.

Jupiter

Neptune

A dwarf planet like Pluto orbits its star (the Sun) and is almost round in shape but other objects enter its orbital area.

Saturn

Uranus

Mercury

Venus

Earth

Mars

The outer planets (Jupiter, Saturn, Uranus, and Neptune) are huge balls of gasses with rings.

The inner planets (Mercury, Venus, Earth, and Mars) are rocky.

Moons (satellites) orbit planets. The Earth has one moon. Mercury and Venus do not have moons. Mars has two moons. Each of the outer planets has many moons. Scientists keep discovering more moons. Some moons have their own atmospheres (Saturn's Titan) and some even have water).

Moons don't make light. They are like mirrors—they bounce (reflect) sunlight back.

A planet's atmosphere is a layer of gases held in place by gravity between the planet and space. Saturn's moon, Titan, is the only known moon with a thick atmosphere. Which have the same or similar atmospheres? Compare and contrast the clouds. Which planets or moons have water?

	Atmosphere	Clouds	Water
Mercury	none	none	none
Venus	carbon dioxide, nitrogen	sulfuric acid	none
Earth	nitrogen, oxygen	water vapor	covers ¾ of planet
Mars	carbon dioxide, nitrogen, argon	water vapor	ice at poles
Jupiter	hydrogen, helium	ammonia	on some moons
Saturn	hydrogen, helium	ammonia	on some moons
Titan	nitrogen, methane	methane	none
Uranus	hydrogen, helium, methane	methane	none
Neptune	hydrogen, helium, methane	methane	none
Pluto	nitrogen, carbon monoxide, methane	nitrogen	none

Mercury, Venus, Earth, and Mars all have volcanoes; as do the moons Io, Enceladus, and Titan.

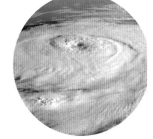

Some planets are hot and some are cold.

Wind speeds vary by planet.

	Temperatures		Wind	
	Fahrenheit	Celsius	miles/hour	km/hour
Sun	around 10,000	around 5,500	1,000,000	1,609,000
Mercury	-279 low to 800 high	-173 low to 427 high	none	
Venus	864 average	462 average	light at surface	
Earth	-126 low to 136 high	-88 low to 58 high	0 to >302 (tornado)	0 to >486 (tornado)
Mars	-125 low to 23 high	-87 low to -5 high	0 to 100	0 to 160
Jupiter	-234 average	-148 average	> 380	> 612
Saturn	-288 average	-178 average	1,000	1600
Uranus	-357 average	-216 average	90 to 360	145 to 580
Neptune	-353 average	-214 average	up to 1500	up to 2400
Pluto	-387 low to -369 high	-233 low to -223 high	unknown	unknown

The Sun: Heat and Light

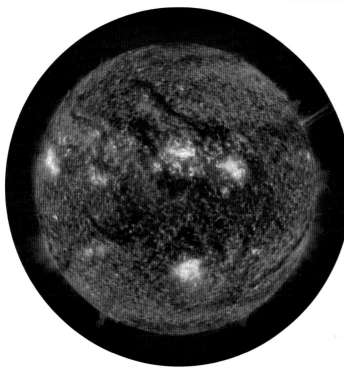

The Sun is the star at the center of our solar system. It is over 4 billion (4,000,000,000) years old. That's a lot of birthday candles!

It is a medium-sized star. It looks so big to us compared to other stars because it is the closest star to us.

The Earth could fit in the Sun about 1 million (1,000,000) times!

You should not stare at the Sun directly as it could hurt your eyes.

It is a huge ball of bubbling and churning gas—you would not be able to stand on it.

Like the planets, the Sun spins on its axis.

The Sun's outer atmosphere (corona) can only be seen during a total eclipse.

Sun Photo Credit: NASA/European Space Agency

The middle of the Sun (core) is very hot and acts like an "energy factory" or nuclear reactor. It creates the heat and light that living things need to survive on Earth.

If you've ever stood by a fire, you know that fire gives off heat and light too. Think of how hot the Sun must be to get that heat and light all the way to Earth! *Do you think the planets closest to the Sun receive more or less heat and light than the planets that are far away from the Sun? Why?*

It takes less than ten minutes for sunlight and heat to reach the Earth—about 93 million (93,000,000) miles (150 million kilometers) away.

Sunspots are cooler, darker areas on the Sun's surface caused by magnetic storms. The Earth could fit into some sunspots!

Solar flares are sudden explosions of intense energy coming out of a sunspot. These flares hit the Earth's atmosphere and can cause radio static and short-wave outages. Coronal Mass Ejections are billion-ton clouds of heated gas (called plasma) that travel at millions of miles per hour from the sun. When they hit Earth they can cause auroras and electrical power blackouts.

Sunspot Loops Photo Credit: Goddard Space Flight Center

Thinking it Through: Life and Basic Needs

In order to survive, living things have basic needs that have to be met in their habitat on their planet. Here on Earth, animals need food, water, oxygen to breathe, and a safe space for shelter and to give birth to their young. Plants need sunlight and heat (temperature), water, soil to grow, and a way for seeds to move (disperse). Even on Earth, life forms look very different from each other. A cactus survives in dry climates and would not survive in the rainforest. Plants and animals that live in cold climates (Arctic, Antarctic, or high elevations) won't survive in the hot tropics. And animals absorb oxygen differently too. As mammals, humans breathe oxygen from the air using lungs. Fish absorb oxygen from the water using gills.

Scientists are looking for possible life in our solar system—whether on other planets or their moons. They don't expect to find life that looks like humans. Many scientists think it is possible that life on other planets (called extra-terrestrial life) could look like living things on Earth that are too small to be seen without a microscope (called microbes). While many microbes, like bacteria, are all around us, there are some microbes that survive in extreme environments here on Earth. For example, microbes live under ice in the Antarctic, in the hot geysers of Yellowstone, in dark underground caves, or even deep in the ocean. There are even a few bacteria that don't need oxygen!

Some scientists are listening for signs of human-like (intelligent) life on planets in other solar systems. By using radio and optical telescopes, these scientists listen or look for radio or light signals sent from other solar systems, hoping to find intelligent life on planets in those solar systems. Scientists also use the telescopes to learn more about the stars and planets beyond our solar system.

If you were to travel to another planet, what would you need to survive? Pick a planet to visit and draw and/or describe what you might need to take with you. How would you get your oxygen? How would you stay warm or cool?	What do YOU think life might look like on another planet? Pick a planet and draw and/or describe a plant or animal that might live on that planet. Without plants to make oxygen for us (using photosynthesis), animals might not have enough oxygen on Earth to breathe. What might plants look like on your planet? In what will they grow? What gas might they make through photosynthesis? What would animals look like? What would they breathe? What would they eat and drink? How would they live? How would they move?

For more activities including Size and Distance and Making a Solar Oven, go to www.SylvanDellPublishing.com, click on the book's cover and then click on Teaching Activities.

To my children, Kaden and Lucy, for always cheering me on—KKW

For BK & JK, who always keep a weather eye out for me—LAK

Thanks to Alice Sarkisian Wessen, Manager, Solar System/Outer Planets & Technology Education and Public Outreach at JPL; Dr. Sten Odenwald, Astrophysicist at Goddard Spaceflight Center and creator of SpaceMath at NASA; and Dr. Stephen Edberg, Astronomer at JPL for checking the accuracy of the information in this book.

Thanks to NOAA for the use of the hurricane image in the For Creative Minds section.

Library of Congress Cataloging-in-Publication Data

Whitt, Kelly Kizer, 1973-
  Solar system forecast / by Kelly Kizer Whitt ; illustrated by Laurie Allen Klein.
    p. cm.
  Audience: Ages 4-9.
  ISBN 978-1-60718-523-9 (hardcover) -- ISBN 978-1-60718-532-1 (pbk.) -- ISBN 978-1-60718-541-3 (English ebook) 1. Solar system--Juvenile literature. 2. Planetary meteorology--Juvenile literature. I. Klein, Laurie Allen, ill. II. Title.
  QB602.W49 2012
  551.50999'2--dc23
                              2012007599

Also available:
    eBooks featuring auto-flip, auto-read, 3D-page-curling, and selectable English and Spanish text and audio
    ISBN: 978-1-60718-560-4.
    Spanish translation: El pronóstico del sistema solar ISBN 978-1-60718-678-6 (hardcover) and
    978-1-60718-550-5 (Spanish eBook)

Interest level: 004-009

Grade level: P-4 Lexile Level: 890

Curriculum keywords: solar system, sun as star, weather

Manufactured in China, June, 2012
This product conforms to CPSIA 2008
First Printing

Sylvan Dell Publishing
Mt. Pleasant, SC 29464